Mice Make TROUBLE

Story by Becky Bloom

Illustrated by Pascal Biet

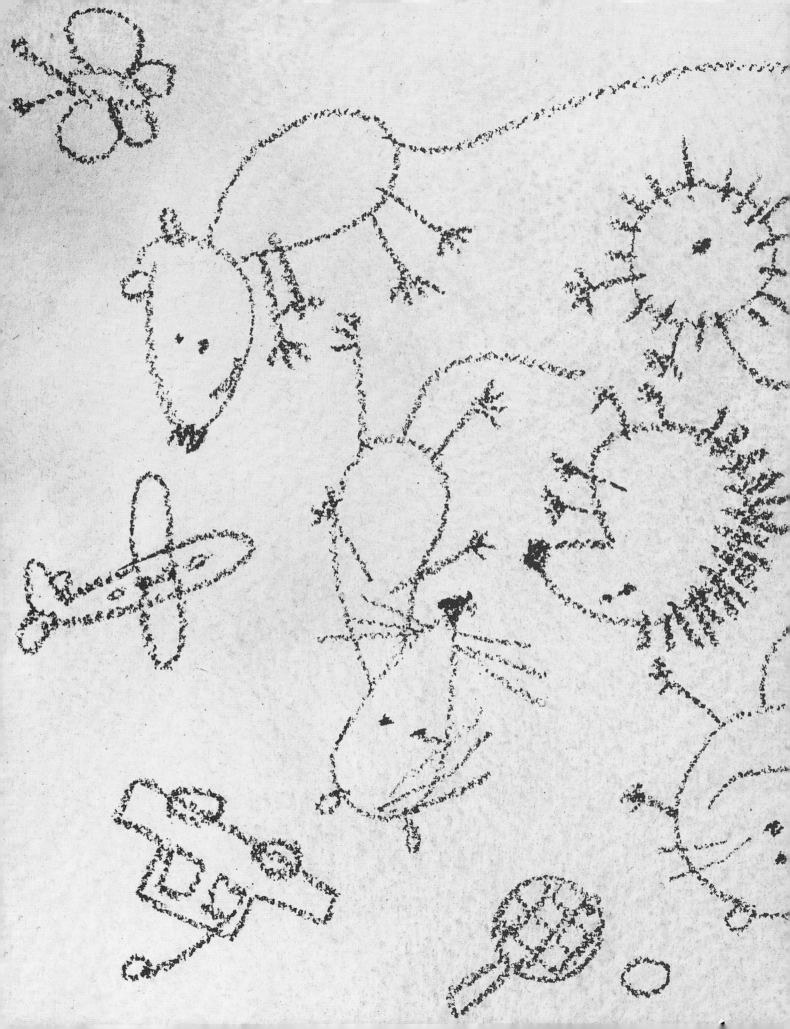

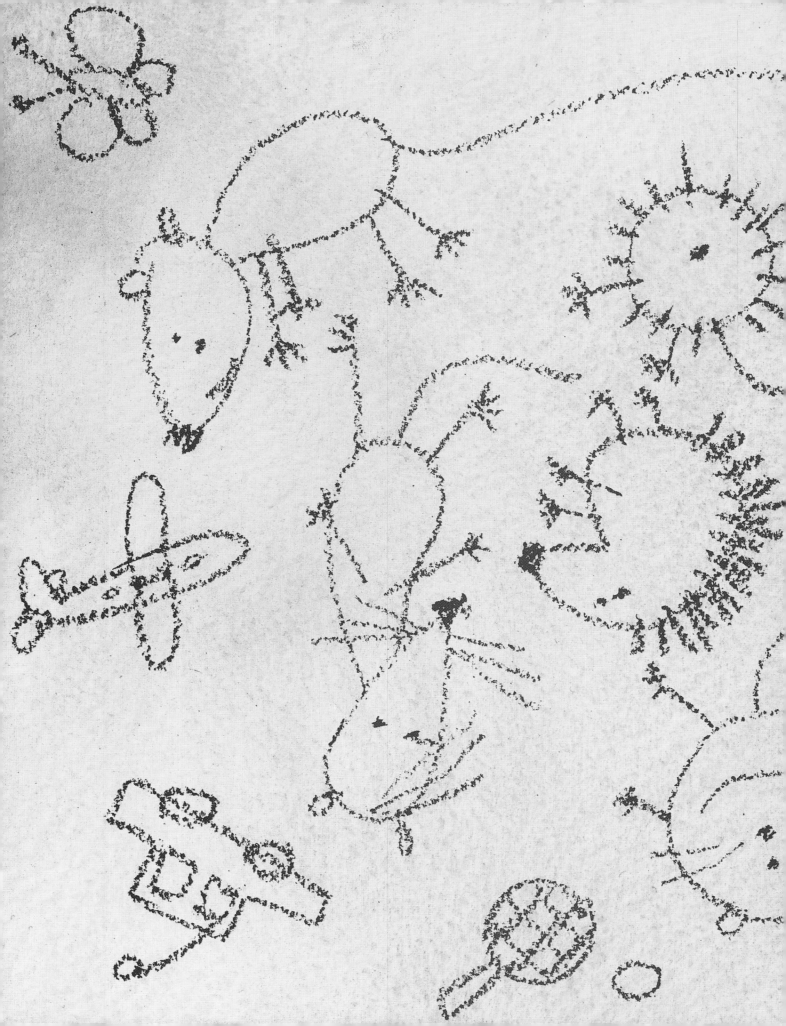

coming
out of
the wall.

After the teacher and the animals left, there were no signs of what had happened, except for the tiny mousehole—which no one had remembered to wipe away.

And sometimes, as Henry lies in bed at night, if he listens carefully, he can still hear chuckling and giggling

Then the
six mice
apologized
to Henry
and went
quietly into the
mousehole.
They dragged
along the hedgehog,
who was quite
reluctant
to leave Henry's
room.

And when all of the toys were put away, the teacher
drew a small cardboard box to hold all the little
animals crawling and flying about the room;
she planned to show them to her kindergarten mice.

Then she had the mice and the hedgehog scrub all of the pencil marks from the walls and the floor and the furniture, and put Henry's room back in order.

But then she looked around Henry's
room and thought it most impolite
to leave him with such a mess.
Taking the colored pencils, she
quickly drew a broom, some soap,
pails of warm water, brushes
and mops.

"Quiet, please!" she said firmly as she walked off the wall, and at once the mice were silent and a little embarrassed. "Come to me, all of you," she instructed, taking the youngest mouse by the hand. She was about to take all of them into the mousehole and keep them busy with nursery rhymes and games.

She was a very serious and respectable mouse-lady, with rimmed glasses and a book in her hand. And she looked just right!

What a mess they were making! Even the hedgehog
contributed: his prickles had torn the pillow to pieces.
Finally Henry had an idea. He grabbed the box of
colored pencils away from the mice and, as
fast as he could, he drew a teacher.

Then he sat on a comfortable pillow and began to read. And that is when the trouble began. Now that the mice had found out about the magic pencils, they started drawing all sorts of toys, all of them entirely inappropriate for indoors. And they jumped and hopped and raced around the room, shrieking and cheering.

He had found the
colored pencils
and was drawing
a glass of soda.

Henry was delighted to have company, but his playmates were not very civilized. They started fighting and soon spoiled the games. Only the hedgehog knew how to behave.

One had too big an ear, another too long a tail, another too round a head. There were red noses, crooked whiskers, long legs, fleecy fur. What an extraordinary assortment of mice they were!

but none of them
seemed to mind at all.

But as the hedgehog walked off the wall to explore Henry's room, the six not-quite-right mice followed right behind. Each one of them had the very problem that had made Henry wipe it away in the first place,

which wasn't right either;
neither was the next one,
or the one after that,
and so on, until six mice
had been wiped away. Henry
finally settled for a hedgehog.
It was much easier to draw.

A mouse!

That was it! Henry quickly sketched a mousehole on
the wall and drew a mouse above it. But the mouse
didn't look quite right, and Henry had to wipe it away
and draw another . . .

and before he had time
to draw anything else
the car popped off the
wall and zoomed across
the room. Henry would
have loved to ride in it, but the
car was way too tiny for him.
Who would be small enough to
get in this car? he wondered.

One day Henry secretly borrowed his sister's box of colored pencils. She had said the pencils were magic, and he wanted to see for himself.

"WARNING: Do not draw dangerous or mischievous animals" was printed on the cover of the box. But Henry couldn't read yet. He closed the curtains in his room and began to draw on the bare wall. He drew a tiny car and colored it red . . .

Mice Make TROUBLE

Story by Becky Bloom

Illustrated by Pascal Biet

SCHOLASTIC INC.
New York   Toronto   London   Auckland   Sydney
Mexico City   New Delhi   Hong Kong   Buenos Aires

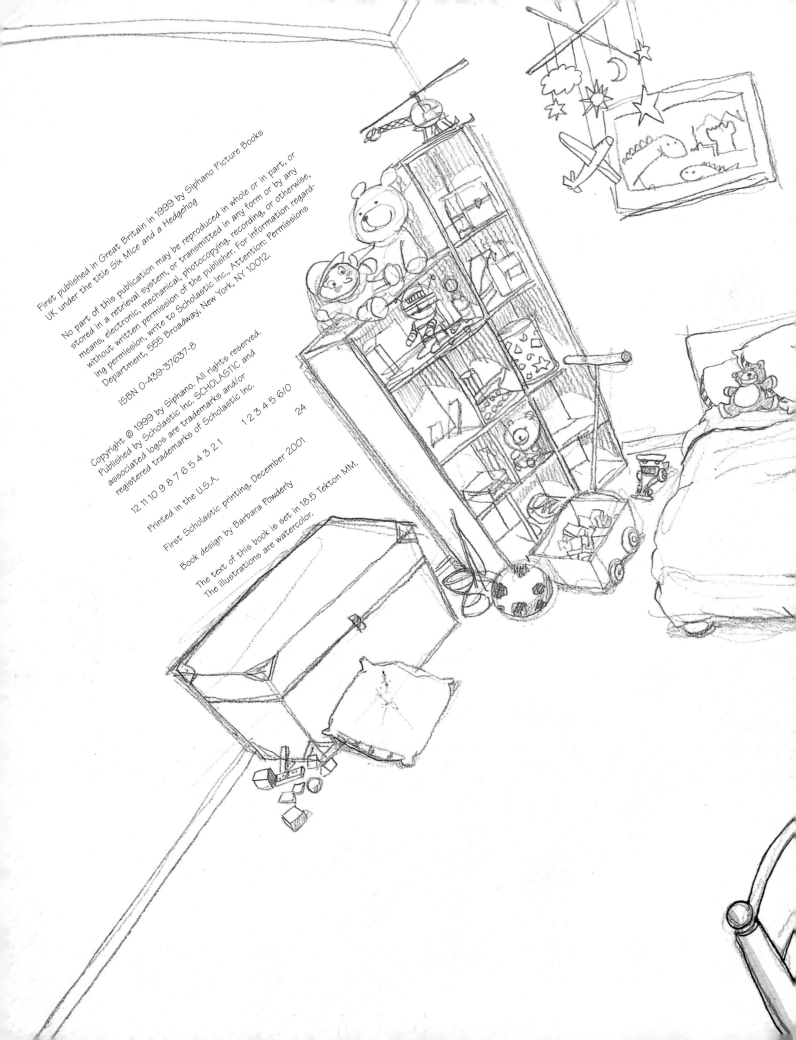